TERRY DEARY

Victorian Tales

Twisted Tunnels

Inside illustrations by
Helen Flook

BLOOMSBURY EDUCATION
AN IMPRINT OF BLOOMSBURY
LONDON OXFORD NEW YORK NEW DELHI SYDNEY

Victorian Tales

Twisted Tunnels

This second edition first published 2016 by
Bloomsbury Education, an imprint of Bloomsbury Publishing Plc
50 Bedford Square, London, WC1B 3DP

www.bloomsbury.com

First published in 2012 by A & C Black Limited.

Bloomsbury is a registered trademark of Bloomsbury Publishing Plc

A CIP catalogue for this book is available from the British Library

ISBN: 978 1 4729 3984 5 (paperback)

Printed and Bound by CPI Group (UK) Ltd, Croydon CR0 4YY

1 3 5 7 9 10 8 6 4 2

Chapter 1

London 25 March 1843

The River Thames oozes along like a green-black slug. Boats and barques, frigates and ferries, wherries and windjammers, clippers, coasters and colliers, steam-tugs, luggers and liners slide up and down the oily river. They don't bob along the waves, like toy yachts on a park pond. No, they sit in the waves like treacle.

And as for the smell... you would not want to smell it. The great river smells of tar and rot, of dead wood and dead horses, foggy smoke that chokes and vinegar that stings your nose.

Most of all it smells of people. People who have never seen a bar of soap, or tasted water that isn't green. People who smell like people who never wash.

The old man scratches his hair under the greasy grey cap. He sniffs the air.

"The river smells fresh today," he says.

The girl at his side would be a princess...

if princesses wore rags that hardly covered their bones, boots that are thick with mud and a face that is a little bit dirtier than a road after a mudslide. She wrinkles her nose. It's a princessy sort of nose... if princesses have noses that curve up at the tip like a warthog's.

"Fresh?" she says and frowns.

"Oh, yes, Jenny. All those lovely little sewers emptying into the River Thames,"

the old man says. "I can smell gold in them sewers."

"You always did have a funny nose, Granddad," she nods.

The old man looks down the long stairway that leads underground. Brass hand-rails gleam and greenish gas lamps glow.

"There you are... the Thames Tunnel. The first tunnel ever built underwater. It's amazing. Amazing, Jenny."

The girl wrinkles her nose. "This is my treat is it? A day off working in the sewers to look at a tunnel. Thanks, Granddad."

The man looked a little hurt. "It's amazing."

"So you said. But to me it's just like the sewers we work in. It's a big hole," she mutters.

"A big hole that lets you cross the river Thames."

"Why would I want to do that?"

"To get to the other side."

She shakes her head sadly. "And they charge you a penny to go in it, you say?"

"A penny is nothing to the posh folk that want to get across the river," he cries, then goes quiet. "Cor, I wish I was posh."

Jenny frowns. "What would you do if you was posh, Granddad?" she asks.

He scowls. "Don't know. Buy a horse and carriage and ride around town. Have lots of servants to light the fire and cook me meals. And have a real nice pair of boots that don't hurt me feet."

Jenny nods again. "But would you still be a tosher? Would you still work in the sewers?" she asks.

He looks at the wide pipes that empty into the river below them. They're like a cave made of shiny red brick.

"Oh, yes, Jenny. I love the sewers. It's a good life. I'd miss my friends if I stopped working in the sewers. If I was riding round in me carriage all day I'd miss you too."

Jenny's little mouth turns down at the corners. "What? Why am I not riding round in the carriage with you?"

Granddad sighs. "Because, Jenny, I'll be a posh geezer in me new boots. I don't want no scruffy little girls in my carriage."

"Thanks," the girl says bitterly. She glances along the footpath towards the smoky city. Suddenly she groans. "Look out, Granddad. The coppers is coming."

Granddad shrugs and says, "So what? We aren't doing nothing wrong. You stay where you are, Jenny lass."

Still she hops from foot to foot, ready to run, as the policeman marches up to her, his boots clattering on the cobbles. He is thin as a broomstick and twice as tall.

"Right you two, move along."

Granddad turns ever so slowly, slow as one of those tugboats on the Thames, and looks the policeman in the eye. "No," he says. "No."

Chapter 2

"No-o?" the policeman cries. "I am ordering you to leave this place immediately. If you do not I will arrest you."

"Like to see you try, Mr Copper," Jenny says. "My Granddad used to be a prize fighter when he was younger. A real bruiser. I bet he could still knock your top hat off your big head."

The policeman's mouth flops and flaps like a fish out of its pond. "You cheeky little gutter-rat," he manages to say. "In a few minutes there will be twenty policemen here. He can't fight twenty of us. And when we arrest you we will throw you into the deepest cellar we have and probably throw away the key."

Jenny is just about to argue fiercely when Granddad steps forward. The policeman jumps back and pulls out a heavy wooden truncheon. It's black and has some very fancy gold lettering on it. Granddad holds up his hand.

"We are not breaking any laws. But me and Jenny will move on if you give us one good reason why we should."

The policeman rests a hand on the rattle that is tucked into his belt. He slides the truncheon back into its leather loop.

"This here is the famous new Thames Tunnel," he says.

"We know that, you dotty bottle-stopper," Jenny sneers.

The policeman raises his nose in the air.

"And today it will be visited by a great person. That great person does not wish to be greeted by a couple of smelly sewer-scavengers."

Jenny's small face is screwed up tighter than a rag ball and she is just about to reply when Granddad steps forwards again. "Who is it?"

"Who's who?" the policeman asks.

"The famous person?"

"It's secret."

Granddad turns to Jenny. "Must be the chief of police," he says.

"Hah," the policeman laughs. "Old Tootle-dum-pattick, we call him. He's not what you call important."

"Must be the Lord Mayor of London," Jenny nods wisely.

"Hah! Cod's-head the Mayor is not as important as he likes to think he is." The policeman smirks, pleased that he's winning the guessing game.

"More important than the Lord Mayor?" Granddad gasps. "That means it must be Queen Victoria."

The policeman looked shocked. "I could not possibly say."

Granddad nods to Jenny.

"It's the queen herself, Jenny. Coming to see our great Thames Tunnel."

"It's not your tunnel," the policeman argues.

"It will be once we pays our pennies to get in."

"Yes, well, you can clear off for an hour till Her Majesty has gone down to inspect it," the policeman says.

He looks up the river to where twenty policemen are marching in step. Behind them a fine carriage is clattering and creaking along behind four fine horses.

People gather on the sides of the streets and call out, "God bless the Queen."

Inside the carriage a small and tubby lady waves her white glove at the crowds. She turns to her lady-in-waiting.

"Yes, yes, God bless me," she says happily. "I just wish God could clear all the traffic for us. The roads are so crowded we're going to be late."

The policeman turns to where Granddad and Jenny had been standing. The path by the river is as empty as a balloon. He takes off his top hat and mops at his hot head with a handkerchief.

"Where did those two villains go, eh?"

Chapter 3

Grandpa and Jenny nod at one another as the policeman talks. As soon as his back is turned they hurry down the gas-lit stairway, taking the steps two at a time, and they scamper into the tunnel.

At the bottom the gloomy tunnel is barred with a gate and a woman sits there with a roll of tickets.

"How did you get down here? We're closed today. Secret visitor."

Granddad takes a deep breath and blows out his chest like a robin. "I know. It's Queen Victoria," he says.

"How did you know that?" the woman asks, mouth gawping open.

"Because I am her sweeper. I go ahead of her and make sure the floors are clean. Very fussy about dusty shoes is young Vic."

The woman's round face was set in a scowl. "Where's your brushes?" she asks.

"I uses me hankie," Granddad says and flicks her desk with it. "Vic won't like that. Better get cleaning, missus."

The woman starts scrubbing around with the sleeve of her grey dress.

Granddad lifts Jenny over the barrier and climbs over it himself. They hurry down the tunnel. There are stalls selling flowers and food, souvenirs and sandwiches. But today they are all closed.

Granddad drags Jenny into the gaslight shadows of a pie stall and they crouch down.

Silence.

Jenny looks at the huge brick tube she finds herself inside. "Cor, Granddad... it's like one of those big churches."

Granddad has seen many wonders in his life but even he looks up in amazement. "A cathedral," he says softly. "A cathedral under the river."

There is a clatter of horse-hoofs and a crunch of marching police boots at the top of the stairs. The queen has arrived.

"Who's that then?" Jenny asks.

"The queen of Great Britain, Queen Victoria," Granddad says. "Come to see our tunnel."

"So what'll she do if she finds us in here?"

"Dunno, Jenny. Maybe send us to the Tower of London and have our heads chopped off."

"Cor, Granddad. You must think I'm a right nickey-chub if you reckon I believe that," Jenny scoffs.

"All the same, those blue-bottle police could arrest us," Granddad argues. "They'll slap the ruffles on your wrists, give you a terrier crop and haul you off to some cold crib. Best hide in one of the small drains till she's cut her ribbon and gone."

The two toshers scrabble and scramble behind the stall. They make it just in time.

A man arrives at the entrance to the tunnel and blows a tune on a trumpet.

"*Parp-parpa-raa, parpa-raa, parpa-raa.*"

It rings round the tunnel like a trumpet played in a tunnel. Which it is.

The policemen form a line of navy blue with bright buttons and boots while the chief of the tunnel company makes a very long and very boring speech.

"This is a proud day for... blah-di-blah-di-blahh..."

(I won't tell you what he says because you'll fall asleep. In fact Queen Victoria is almost falling asleep. Granddad is dozing and even Jenny feels her eyes begin to close.)

At last... at long, long last... the queen steps forward and simply says, "We are happy to be here."

The policemen clap their hands but as they have gloves on, it sounds like the patter of rain on a wood-rotted roof.

Then the queen walks forward until she is alongside the pie stall where Jenny is hiding.

"How far does this tunnel go?" she asks the chief of the sewer company.

"Over four hundred yards, your highness."

The queen sighs. "I wish there was a tunnel all the way to Buckingham Palace. I could have my coachman drive me home in half an hour. It would save me hours in all that traffic."

And Jenny can't stop herself. She knows she shouldn't say a word. But she does.

"You'd be even quicker in a train, your queenship," she says.

"Who said that?" Victoria squawks.

"Me. I'm behind here," Jenny says, poking her thin nose out. "You're not going to chop me head off, are you?"

"I wouldn't chop off such a clever young head," the queen says, looking up. "I have never heard such a clever idea. Imagine tunnels like this under London. We could have trains running along them all day and no old carts and carriages to slow them down. What a good idea. I'm glad I thought of it."

The queen turns round and bustles out of the tunnel. "Send for Charles Pearson. Have him at the palace tomorrow. I want him to build an underground railway.

The London Underground Railway. What an idea. What a wonderful queen I am."

Granddad moans, "I can't believe you just spoke to our mighty queen."

"Our mighty thieving queen," Jenny says.

"Thieving? What's she nicked?"

"She's only gone and pinched my great idea," Jenny sighs.

"Ideas is not worth a penny. Time to go," Granddad says. "Back to our sewers. Time to make ourselves rich as rich."

Chapter 4

17 years later: February 1860

Jenny wakes in her warm bed.

"Rich as rich," Granddad had promised her, and rich as rich they are – for poor folk. She's a fine young woman now but still she works in the sewers. Granddad is older and slower now. She can't leave him.

So every day they go into the sewers and plunge their hands into the muck to find their treasures. Some they sell and some they keep.

It's odd what ends up down the drains: rings and watches, golden pens and silver shoe buckles. "Finders keepers," Granddad says. "Half for me and half for Jenny. Fair's fair."

The coins they spend on coal for their fire and best beef for their broth, tea and buttered muffins and cake and jellied eels. They live well in their little room near to King's Cross Railway Station.

The other people in the house are poor as mice and many live by stealing. Granddad guards their treasure well. Burglars try, but never find it.

Best of all Jenny likes the warm blankets to keep out the winter chills in their damp and rotting wooden building. They share one room, like everyone else in the tall and tumbling house. But they are snug.

This morning Jenny wonders why she woke so early. It's the noise outside in the street. People are shouting and swearing, crying and complaining, boiling with bitterness.

She scrapes the ice off the inside of the window and looks through. Half the street is up while the sun is still not out of bed. They are crowding around the end of the row of houses, pointing at something.

"What's going on, Granddad?" she asks.

Granddad doesn't answer, because Granddad isn't there. His bed is empty and his clothes are gone.

Jenny pulls on her boots and her coat and shawl. She hurries down the creaking stairs where it's too dark to see the dogs and cats and spiders and rats that scurry out of her way.

The street is frosted and the wind is sharp as an icicle. Jenny sees Granddad – red-nosed in the cold and red-faced with

anger. He's jabbing a finger at a poster that's pasted on the wall.

"What's happening, Granddad?"

He sighs. "See for yourself," he moans.

"Don't be a bufflehead, Granddad. I never learned to read. You always said you'd teach me," she reminds him.

He nods. "It says they are building one of the new underground railway lines along this street."

She shrugs. "You mean *under* this street. Don't bother me."

"No, no, it *will* bother you. You see, they dig up the whole street and keep digging down till they have a huge trench. It'll be wide enough to take two trains. Then they drop in the railway lines, put brick walls up the sides and put a roof on. They finish off by putting the road back on top."

Suddenly the crowd of angry people start to run to the far end of the street. Ten huge carts are rolling towards them. Each is pulled by four mighty horses and all are filled with workmen carrying shovels and pick-axes.

Jenny can make out cries of, "Get out of it ... you're not digging up our street."

The men, women and children make a circle round the wagons and try to stop the workers climbing down.

Then they hear the blast of whistles – police whistles. Fifty bobbies bound down from the last wagon in the line. They draw out their black, hardwood sticks and use them to beat back the mob. The bruised and bleeding limp home to heal their hurts.

Jenny just shakes her head. "Granddad ... the street's wide enough for one train. But they'll never get *two* trains in, side by side."

Granddad sighs. "I know, my little sparrow. That's what the notice says. They have to knock down one side of the street. Flatten half the houses."

"I can see why everybody's so unhappy, Granddad. But which side of the street are they going to knock down?"

The man's eyes are dull as the winter sky. "Our side, Jenny. Our side."

Chapter 5

Another year and a bit later, March 1861

Jenny and Granddad wander the bleak streets for weeks. Every house is full of families fleeing the mud-munching monster of the underground railway.

At last they find a tiny attic room in a house in the north of London. Every day it takes them hours to walk to the river to be toshers in the slosh of the sewers.

They tosh and search for a while each day. Too soon it is time to head home. In the dark days of winter there is hardly light for two hours of toshing. Slowly their fat purses shrink. And one day they are empty except for Jenny's few pennies.

That's the day Granddad is walking back from the cold and clammy Thames and he says, "Tell you what, Jenny. Let's pack in the toshing."

"What'll we do to live, Granddad?"

"We'll get jobs."

"Jobs? Who'll have a girl like me? Who'll want an old pudding head like you?"

Granddad grins a pink-gummed grin. 'The railways, Jenny, the railways. There are lots of jobs for a strong man like me – loading the wagons, shovelling the coal, carrying the cases for the posh passengers – they call that job a porter. They say they pay two shillings a day. And we get to smell a lot sweeter too. Why, you could smell like a rosebud and then find yourself a nice young man maybe."

Jenny scowls. "I don't like rotten roses .. and young men are boring. You've seen them in the sewers, Granddad, splashing around and playing hide-and-seek in the tunnels when they should be looking for silver and gold."

Granddad nods. "I know, girl, but you are like a gold pocket-watch in a sewer – a rare and precious find. They can't all be like you."

"But what do I do when you are out portering for posh passengers?" Jenny cries.

"I've thought of that," the man chuckles. "don't you worry. You see, with all these trains bringing people to London from everywhere, the passengers need places to stay. There's lots of hotels being built near the stations. You, my girl, can easy get a job as a maid."

"What? *Serving* people?" Jenny sighs and wrinkles her thin nose in disgust.

"Change their bed clothes, do the laundry, serve their food and sweep their rooms. They pay you, they feed you in the hotel kitchen *and*, if the posh people's pleased, they give you tips as well. And... *and*... here's the thing... they sometimes give their maids rooms in the hotel attics to sleep. Save you all this travelling."

"You mean, *not* live with you Granddad?" she gasps. "I can't remember not living with you."

"You're a grown woman, Jen. You don't need me to look after you."

Jenny's mouth falls open in surprise. "I know that. I know *that*. But you need *me* to look after *you*."

The old man shrugs. "They say the rail workers can have special lodgings near the station. I get a job at King's Cross, you get a job at the King's Cross Hotel, and we can see each other every day after work."

"No more toshing?" she asks.

"No more toshing."

"No more sewers?"

"No more sewers. And no more worries about where the next crust of bread will come from."

Jenny walks a little further, thinking hard. Finally she says, "So, Granddad, do I have to be polite to these posh people?"

"Oh, yes," he tells her.

She blows out her lips. "That'll be the hardest bit, Granddad."

"I know," he says. "I know."

Chapter 6

Another two years later
Saturday, January 10, 1863

Jenny looks in the mirror and hardly knows the girl who stares back. Her clean, brown hair is shining and tied in a neat black bow. A bright white apron covers a black woollen dress and her black shoes shine clear as a robin's eyes. She shares the attic with five other hotel maids but she knows she is the smartest.

The morning frost covers her window. There is a sharp knock on the door to the

room then it opens. A man in a suit and top hat stands there flapping his hands. "Jenny, oh Jenny, save my life."

Jenny smiles. "Yes, Mr Burbage?" She knows the hotel manager always sees terror in a teacup and disaster in a dustpan. "What can I do for you, sir?" she asks.

"The new underground railway opens today."

"Yes, sir, I know."

"There is to be a small party at Buckingham Palace – the queen is having lunch with the men who built it. The chef from the King's Cross hotel has been asked to cook. A great honour for us all. We sent two serving maids but they need another."

Jenny gathers her coat and says, "Your secret is safe, sir. But how will I get across London in time? The streets are jammed with people."

"You will take the underground train," Mr Burbage says as he shoos the girl down the servants' stairs towards the railway station. "A special train. An empty coach is waiting to travel to Paddington and a coach will drive you to the palace from there. They are waiting for you."

"For me?" Jenny laughs and claps her hands. "So I'll be the first passenger ever to travel on the underground."

"You will. Another honour for us."

Jenny shrugs. "No more than I deserve. After all, it was my idea."

Mr Burbage frowns. "I think you will find it was Queen Victoria's idea, Jenny."

And Jenny just smiles.

The stairway down to the platform is long and smells of smoke from the steaming train. Mr Burbage opens a carriage door and the fine new seats are cosier than a cat's basket. "You can ride first class, Jenny," the manager says.

"Quite right too," Jenny tells him. "Today I'll be a posh person... the poor have to make do with the open trucks. Today I shall be a lady."

Mr Burbage shakes his head. "You are behaving very strangely today, girl. You are not going to let me down in front of the queen, are you?"

Jenny says nothing. But Jenny thinks, "Wait and see."

The tunnels are quite light with long shafts leading up to the road above, letting out the smoke and letting in the light. The

white tiles on the shafts dazzle under the frost-blue January sky above. Jenny looks out as they pass through a station, raises her voice to shout above the clanking noise.

"What are those black bags?"

"Dead bodies," Mr Burbage says with a shudder. We're passing under the old cemetery. They haven't quite finished moving all the bodies to a new one outside the city."

"It must have been a cemetery for the poor," Jenny sighs. "The rich would never let their corpses be shuffled around like bags of bones in a butcher shop."

"You *are* going to let me down in front of the queen, aren't you?" Mr Burbage groans. "Remember, her dearest husband Albert died two years ago and she still wears black. She doesn't need a serving girl upsetting her."

Jenny laughs. "I'll behave."

Mr Burbage peers out of the window, "Ah, here we are. At Paddington. Let's go up to the street for your coach. It seems the queen needs some help with her robes. Someone to carry them as she walks down the stairs to the lunch."

"I can do that," Jenny says. "I've been wanting a word with her for a couple of years now," she mutters to herself.

Chapter 7

Queen Victoria looks in a mirror and likes what she sees. Her doctor says she looks round as a beer-barrel but the queen's fine black dress tucks her in.

She reads the speech she is going to give to the twenty people in the grand room below.

"*We wish to praise you on this day. The first day of our wonderful underground railway.*"

The door opens and Jenny walks in.

"*Just twenty years ago we visited the Thames Tunnel.*" The queen stops and looks at Jenny. "Ah, you girl, help us on with this velvet cloak." Then the queen goes on with her speech. "*And when we visited the tunnel we had a wonderful idea. Let us have more tunnels filled with railways.*"

Jenny lifts the cloak onto the queen's shoulders, "But that's not quite true, is it your majesty?"

"What? Do I know you, girl?"

"You met me in the sewer nearly twenty years ago," Jenny reminds her.

"You were the smelly urchin girl? And I said we should have roads under the city."

"Yes," Jenny agrees. "For *carriages*. And *I* said, 'You'd be even quicker in a train, your queenship'."

"Maybe you did," the queen mutters and her pale face turns pink.

"And there are a lot of poor people who don't like you," Jenny says. She knows she'll upset the queen – she knows she promised not to – but she can't stop herself. "Quite a few have tried to kill you, haven't they?"

"They have. Are you another?" the queen asks, and her voice trembles.

"No. I'm just *telling* you, those wonderful trains drove a lot of poor people out of their homes, put a lot of them out of work... even put dead paupers out of their coffins. Us poor people hate the railway for that."

"And... and if I say I invented the railway they'll hate me?"

"Even more than they do already." Jenny nods. "The next person that tries to kill you may succeed."

Now Victoria is pale again. "So you think I should keep quiet about my part in making the underground railway?"

"*Our* part," Jenny says as she fastens the bow at the front of the cloak. She steps behind and lifts the trailing cloak.

"There you are, your queenship, ready to go. Have a nice meal."

Queen Victoria picks up her speech and tears the paper into pieces. They head through the door and stand at the top of the fine stairway. "I was looking forward to telling people I invented this railway."

"That's just boasting, your queenship," Jenny tells her. "You can try it... but I'll just stand up and tell them the truth."

Victoria looks over her shoulder. "You would, too."

"I would, too," Jenny grins.

Victoria begins to walk down the stairs to where the guests are waiting, clapping their hands for their queen.

The queen sighs. "Twenty years ago, in that tunnel..." she says.

"Yes?" Jenny asks.

"Maybe I *should* have had your head cut off."

Jenny laughs. "Maybe you should, your queenship. Maybe you should."

True History

The 'Big Stink' brought misery to London in 1858. The city built eighty miles of sewers to carry waste to the Thames River. There is a story that Queen Victoria was so excited about the new sewer tunnels that she ordered a small rail line to be built inside the great sewer. It could take people on little trips. She had invented the London Underground.

The truth is the idea for a line under the ground from Paddington Station to King's Cross was first put forward in 1854... five years before

Victoria opened the great sewer. So we don't know if the story of Victoria 'inventing' the underground is true... but it's a good story.

The London Underground was a great success when it opened in 1863, but at a terrible cost to the poorest people of London. They had their homes pulled down to make the tunnels. Even graveyards were moved to make way for the railway lines.

Not all of the British people liked Queen Victoria and, in her lifetime, seven people tried to kill her. One of her Prime Ministers, Benjamin Disraeli, said that Victoria wasn't

queen of ONE country. Disraeli said Britain was TWO nations – two groups of people who did not understand each other and did not like each other. The two nations were the Rich and the Poor.

The 'toshers' who hunted in the sewage for something valuable were the poorest of the poor. Victoria was the richest of the rich – but spent most of her life being miserable after her husband Albert died in 1861.

You try

1. If you were a treasure hunter what FIVE things would YOU like to find buried on the land or under the muddy banks of a river?

2. Queen Victoria may have given the underground railway idea to the railway companies. Can you write a letter from the excited queen to Mr Brunel, the great tunnel and railway builder, telling him about your great invention?

3. The Victorian people had a lot of fun making up nasty names for the people they didn't like. Insults. The made up words like these in the story...

> *Bufflehead*
> *Gutter-rat*
> *Tootle-dum-pattick*
> *Nickey-chub*
> *Cod's-head*

Why not work with a friend and see who can come up with the FIVE funniest new insults?